Henry and Mudge

AND

Annie's Good Move

The Eighteenth Book of Their Adventures

Story by Cynthia Rylant
Pictures by Suçie Stevenson

SCHOLASTIC INC.

New York Toronto London Auckland Sydney
Mexico City New Delhi Hong Kong

For Dawna and Sam—CR
For Jane and Emily Stevenson—SS

ISBN 0-590-04053-7

Published by Scholastic Inc., 555 Broadway, New York, NY 10012,
by arrangement with Simon & Schuster Books for Young Readers,
Simon & Schuster Children's Publishing Division. READY-TO-READ
is a registered trademark of Simon & Schuster.
SCHOLASTIC and associated logos are trademarks and/or registered
trademarks of Scholastic Inc.

12 11 10 9 8 7 6 5 4 3 2 1   1 2 3 4 5/0

Printed in the U.S.A.   24

First Scholastic printing, March 2000

The text of this book was set in 18-point Goudy.
The illustrations were rendered in pen-and-ink and watercolor.

Contents

Next Door!

Henry and Henry's big dog Mudge
always liked visits from Henry's
cousin Annie.
She was very careful about things,
like her frilly dresses and her shiny shoes.
But she was fun.

She liked Henry,
she liked Mudge,
and she could throw
a mean Frisbee.

So when Henry's mother
said one day that Annie was
moving, and that she was
moving *next door* to Henry,
Henry was thrilled!

"We have to help Annie move,"
Henry told Mudge.
"You know how careful she is,"
Henry said. "I bet she'll
be nervous."

Henry imagined Annie packing
up her things.
"I bet she wraps those shiny
shoes a million times,"
Henry told Mudge.
Mudge wagged.

"And those frilly dresses
a *zillion* times,"
said Henry.
Mudge wagged again.

"Her house is probably
a *mess* right now,"
said Henry.
Mudge wagged and drooled
all over Henry's shoes.

"But not as much of a mess
as I am," said Henry,
looking down.

14

Blotchy

When Henry and Mudge and
Henry's parents
got to Annie's house
on moving day,
Uncle Ed was carrying boxes,
and Annie was breaking out.

15

"Hi, Annie," said Henry.

"You're all blotchy."

"I know," said Annie.

"I break out when I'm nervous."

"Are you nervous about
leaving friends?" asked Henry.
Annie nodded.

"Are you nervous about
changing schools?" asked Henry.
Annie nodded again.

"Are you nervous about all
your frilly dresses
and shiny shoes and
lace hankies being on that truck?"
asked Henry.
Annie nodded really hard.
Three new blotches came out
on her nose.

"Hmmm," said Henry.
"Do you know what I do when
I get nervous?"
"What?" asked Annie.
"I crawl under the covers
with Mudge," said Henry.
"Do you have
any covers left?"

"No." Annie shook her head.
"They're all on the truck."

"Hmmm," said Henry.

"There are some blankets
on the backseat of our
car. Do you want to use them?"

Annie nodded and smiled.
Henry opened the car door
and Annie got under
the covers.
Mudge wagged and disappeared
under the covers, too.

Henry rolled down the windows
and closed the door.
"Good-bye, blotches!" he called.
And he went to help Uncle Ed.

24

The New House

Annie and Mudge stayed under
the covers all morning long.
Henry brought them food.

He brought them drinks.

He even brought them

a moving man.

The moving man told Annie he
would be very careful with her
shoes and dresses and lace hankies.
A few of her blotches went away.

When the truck was loaded,
everyone drove to Annie's
new house: *next door* to Henry's house!

Then the movers started carrying
the boxes in.

Annie was still under the covers
in the car.
Henry peeked inside.
She was sleeping on a lace hanky
on Mudge's head.

When all of the boxes were
unloaded, the movers went away.
Then Henry woke up Annie, and
everyone went into the new house.

Annie held onto Mudge and
tried not to break out.

"Before we unpack," said
Henry's mother, "we have to make
a new-house wish. We'll wish
for something good for Annie
and Uncle Ed. Something good
for them in their new house."
Annie smiled.
"Great!" said Henry.

Henry's father lit a candle.
"Everyone make a secret wish,"
he said, "then Annie will blow
out the candle."

One by one they wished.

Some wishes were big.

Some were small.

Some looked like T-bone steak.

But they were all good wishes.

Annie blew out the candle.

"Welcome home, Cousin," said Henry.

"Welcome home, Annie," said
Henry's parents.

Mudge gave Annie a great big kiss.

And all of Annie's blotches

went away.

Then the next morning . . .
Henry had breakfast
at *her* house!